PiRATE
Blunderbeard
WORST. MISSION. EVER.

Join Pirate Blunderbeard on more adventures:

Pirate Blunderbeard
WORST. PIRATE. EVER.

Pirate Blunderbeard
WORST. VACATION. EVER.

Pirate Blunderbeard
WORST. MISSION. EVER.

Coming Soon

Pirate Blunderbeard
WORST. MOVIE. EVER.

PIRATE Blunderbeard

WORST. MISSION. EVER.

AMY SPARKES & BEN CORT

HarperCollins *Children's Books*

Mom

Blackbeard

Blunderbeard

Dread Pirate Madlocks

Lazy Jim

Boris

Uncle Redbeard

Redruth

Captain Chomp

Grandad Graybeard

First published in Great Britain by
HarperCollins *Children's Books* in 2018
First published in the United States of America in this edition by
HarperCollins *Children's Books* 2019
HarperCollins *Children's Books* is a division of HarperCollins*Publishers* Ltd,
HarperCollins Publishers
1 London Bridge Street
London SE1 9GF

The HarperCollins website address is:
www.harpercollins.co.uk
1

ISBN 978–0–00–830827–8

Typeset in Bembo MT Schoolbook 15pt/26pt
Printed and bound in the United States of America by LSC Communications

For Alex and Izzy
And for the real GG—with thanks
for all the adventures x

Amy Sparkes is donating a percentage of
her royalties to ICP Support, aiming for
every ICP baby to be born safely.

Reg. charity no. 1146449
www.icpsupport.org

JANUARY 1st

Heading off with Grandpa Graybeard and Cousin Redruth to sail the Seven Seas!

Hurrah!

We'll be out on the waves ... Sun on my face ... Salt in the air ...

We can set up the deck chairs and have ice cream. Mmm, mint chocolate for me! Think I've got some Chick-O-Snacks-flavored popsicles in the freezer for Boris.

Maybe we'll stop off at interesting places. Ooh—I could get a new pirate hat for me and a bucket and spade for Boris.

Here are my New Year's resolutions:

1. Stop biting nails—
THIS TIME I **WILL** DO THIS.

2. Teach Boris how to be a homing chicken.
(She could take postcards to my brother
Blackbeard—he'll be so jealous when he
reads about our travels. Haha.)

3. Survive an adventure with Redruth and
Grandpa Graybeard. I hope.

This ... is going to be **great!**

Or not.

Grandpa has written these New Year's resolutions in MY diary by mistake!!!

1. Teach the lily-livered kids a thing or two about pirating!

2. Face death and danger on the Seven Seas (and be back in time for me evening rum)!

3. Risk life and limb and settle me "business" with THE BOSS once and for all.

What in the name of Neptune's nasal hair does THAT mean?! Probably that I'm in for a year of adventure and disaster—with as much chance of reaching December in one piece as Boris has of being a world-famous limbo dancer ...

JANUARY 20TH

We dropped anchor in the middle of the sea.

Then I dropped Boris in the middle of the sea.

All because Redruth crept up behind me and blasted her PortaCannon™ while

Boris and I were looking out for boats
selling ice cream.

So, nope.

Not my fault at all.

Boris reckons it's my fault.

Grandpa hasn't said *why* we've stopped.
Just that he's got a plan.

OK.... A plan. Sounds ... interesting.

Except "interesting" in my life is not
usually good.

6:30a.m.

AAAARGH!! Grandpa just woke me up by
dumping a bucket of cold, rotten fish over
me and shouting:

"Wake up, ye lazy, lily-livered limpet!
It be Day One of Proper Pirate Training!
HAARRRRRRR!"

Blargh!!! Just spat a
rotten fish-tail out of my
mouth. It be Proper What?!

Grandpa has gone off
dancing a hornpipe and
humming a sea shanty.

Not good.

6:30p.m.

Ouch. Sword. Fight.

Hours. And. Hours.

Redruth. Strong. Me. Not.

Arm. Ache. Pooped.

Bed. Argh. Forgot.

Rotten. Fish. Yuck. Bed.

Squelch.

FEBRUARY 2ND

6:30a.m.

AAAARGH!!

Rotten fish on face.

"Wake up, ye dozy dogfish! It be Day Two of Proper Pirate Training!"

Oh. Please. NO!!!!!

6:30p.m.

Rigging. Climbing. Hate. Heights. Fell. Lots. Water. Wet. Totally. Pooped. Bed.

Argh.

Fish.

FEBRUARY 3RD

6:30a.m.

Slept with umbrella over face.

Rotten fish.

"Get up, ye sluggish sea cucumber! It be Day Three of training."

6:30p.m.

Pretending. Capture. Ships. All. Day. Squelch. Really. Should. Clean. Bed. Now.

FEBRUARY 9TH

6:30a.m.

Day Nine.

Rotten fish.

Please, for the love of cupcakes, someone make this awful training stop!

WHAT'S IT FOR ANYWAY??!!!!

6:30a.m.

Day Seventeen.

Rotten tomatoes.

Grandpa's run out of rotten fish.

He keeps dancing the hornpipe and muttering, "We'll show the Boss."

Day Twenty-eight.

SAVE ME. ☹

MARCH 1ST

8a.m.

Overslept.

Overslept?!

No rotten food on the

face today?! Training's

finally over?

All quiet (except for

Boris snoring).

What's going on?

4p.m.

Grandpa just called me and Redruth up on to the deck and explained everything. He was jiggling around as if he had an electric eel in his trousers.

And clapping his hands, all excited.

"HAHARRR!" he boomed. "Me hearties, we be off to meet our fate!"

Redruth said, "Totally excellent," at the same time as I said, "Fate?! OUR?!"

Turns out "the dreaded Boss" is the

nickname of the scariest pirate on the seas. And that's coming from Grandpa. His real name is Dread Pirate Madlocks and a few years ago he stole Grandpa's ship and made him walk the plank. That's how Grandpa got stranded on the Island of No Return (although he was a bit embarrassed about it all and spread rumors that his ship had gone down in a storm).

Now Grandpa has left the Island of No Return, he wants his old ship back. And he thinks Redruth and I are just the pirates to help him.... Yes, we're on a mission to steal a ship from THE SCARIEST PIRATE ON THE SEAS.

If I may say just one thing? ...

HEEEEEEELP!

HEEEEEEELP!

Why do I get the feeling we are heading

for big,

BIG,

BIG,

BIG trouble?

Oh dear. Oh very dear.

Redruth just showed me Pirate Madlocks

in the "Who's Who" section of her *Pirate*

Monthly magazine.

HEEEEEEELP!
HEEEEEEELP!

WHO'S WHO ON THE SEVEN SEAS

This month: Pirate Madlocks

Hangs out: Somewhere/anywhere on the Seven Seas, stealing your ship

Likes: Ship-stealing, bone-breaking, sword-fighting

Dislikes: Idiots, pesky little pirates

Awards won include:

- *Pirates United Swordfighters* (PUS):
  Best Swordfighter every year since the award started. (He fights anyone

who asks him to hand the trophy back so they decided it was safer to just let him keep it.) Barber Rossa's **Craziest Hair of the Year Award.**

- *Pirate Monthly*'s **Scariest Pirate Who We Are Seriously Impressed With Award.** Twice.

Pirate Pet: Vicious sea-dog called Whoopsie.

Pirate Monthly's **Awesomely Dangerous Pirate Rating:** 10/10

Dislikes idiots? And pesky little pirates?! GULP.

Grandpa came and joined us on deck and sang this sea shanty:

"The dreaded Boss, he rules the seas,
Heave ho, me crazy crew,
Ye'll be a-crawling on yer knees,
Heave ho, good luck to you!

The oceans roared, the cannons boomed,
Heave ho, me crazy crew,
Now we're lost and really doomed.
Heave ho, good luck to you!"

Marvelous.

We are sailing full speed ahead to our certain doom. (Although I'm sure Grandpa doesn't quite know where he's going and no one else seems at all worried! This. Is. Not. Good.)

OK. ... I hate having to do this. But I'm going to contact *The Pirates Against Rubbish Piracy Society* (PARPS). Surely they'll have to do something about a pirate putting his crew in danger? Maybe they'll stop this VOYAGE OF DOOM or whatever it is, rescue me, and then I can just go home and bake some cakes in peace?!

Boris can take the message. I'll just train

her as a homing chicken. I KNEW that
resolution would come in handy.

What can possibly go wrong?

APRIL 3RD

OK…. LOTS.

More later when I've put out the fire.
And cleaned cupcakes off the cabin ceiling.

And gotten Boris's
head unstuck
from the teapot.

Took Boris up on deck, sat her on my shoulder, then let her fly free!

Thought she might fly around over the sea for a couple of minutes, then come back.

She's now sitting up in the crow's nest and refusing to come down.

Oh. That. Chicken!! How many pirates in the history of EVER have had to stand at the bottom of the mast pleading with a chicken?! ☹

Redruth laughed for an hour.

Forget the whole thing. I'm sending PARPS a message in a bottle.

I need to get out of this VOYAGE OF DOOM as soon as possible!

9a.m.

So the only bottle I could find was this: Boris's medicine—

that makes bunged-up chickens poop!! How embarrassing does my life have to be??

I was just trying to decide what to do with the liquid inside the bottle when

ChickaPoo

100%

Fast acting!

Redruth walked in and asked what it was. NO WAY was I telling her that it was "the leading brand of constipation medicine for today's stressed-out chicken." I told her it was a vitamin drink I'm taking so that I'll be on top form when we meet Dread Pirate Madlocks. Redruth did that raise-one-eyebrow-and-put-her-head-on-one-side thing she does when she doesn't believe me so I guzzled the lot. In one go.

No wonder Boris turns the color of seaweed when she drinks it!! YUCK! And if that's not bad enough, I have to keep running to the—

Uh-oh. Back in a sec.

9:30a.m.

Where was I? Oh yeah. I have to keep

running to the—

Hang on.

9:50a.m.

To the—

10:15a.m.

I—

10:30a.m.

Hate—

10:45a.m.

Redruth.

3p.m.

Phew. Oh, my tummy! Think I'm OK now.

I can't BELIEVE I'm writing to PARPS using a bottle that helps chickens poop ☹. But I need them to rescue us from this doomed mission. Maybe they won't notice....

Dear PARPS,

When I wrote to you last year, it is possible I may have been a teensy bit rude. To be fair, you had stranded me on the awful Island of No Return, and I was feeling smug as I'd just rescued myself by getting a lift with Grandpa Graybeard....

However, it turns out I'm in a little trouble. Grandpa is very excited. He's taking us on a mission to get his ship back. On this mission he reckons we will 'meet our fate"—a fate of the "cursed and really doomed" type. This is his idea of FUN!! Surely, he can't be allowed to put his crew in danger?? This must count as lousy pirating? Please???? So I should be allowed to leave the mission, right? Like, now??

Very much hoping you might come and sort of rescue me, before the whole "cursed and doomed" bit.

Yours, more respectfully,

Barnacles Blunderbeard

Inventor, Senior Tester,

Chief Executive, Baker

Blunderbeard's WonderWeird Contraptions

I can see Blackbeard's parrot, Ironclaw!
He's coming this way! He's bringing a
message in his beak! I'm saved! I'm saved!
I'm—

Argh!

He pooped

in my eye.

Fiendish beast!!

May your beak go blunt!!

Opening letter now. Yay! When are they

coming to rescue me?

Pirates **A**gainst **R**ubbish **P**iracy **S**ociety

The Best Pirate Ship in the World

Dead Man's Cove

The Ocean

April 28th

Dear Blunderbeard,

Hahahahahahaha!!!!!! No chance.

Enjoy "meeting your fate."

Yours sincerely,

Blasterous Blackbeard

(Director of PARPS)

P.S. I can't believe you actually used a bottle of <u>chicken poop medicine</u> to contact us! It took ages to reach us. Haven't you heard of homing parrots?? Pirates haven't used bottles for about one hundred years! PARPS feel that your old-fashioned and insulting action (chicken poop??!!) is simply unacceptable and that this is another example of YOUR lousy pirating. Just because you've gone off with Grandpa Graybeard, don't think you're a proper pirate now. You're not, Blunderbeard. Proper pirates DON'T NEED RESCUING!!! Idiot.

Ohhhh dear.

8a.m.

Right. These are my options:

1) ~~Run away~~ (Redruth would find me).

2) ~~Boris and I lead a mutiny and take over the ship~~ (Redruth has her PortaCannon™ and she's a bit scary).

3) Try to get Grandpa's old ship back from Madlocks.

Poo.

Oh no! Boris! I didn't mean——! All over my diary! Oh. That. Chicken! I'll get a cloth. ☹

MAY 30TH

10a.m.

Grandpa is mad because he still can't figure out where Madlocks is at the moment.

I'm staying out of his way and working on homing chicken training for the completely useless Boris. Then she can take a letter to Mom and tell her about the trouble I'm in! Maybe Mom can help.

Blunderbeard's WonderWeird Contraptions are proud to present the …

HenHomer™

Fishing rod

"Arm" for pulling back catapult seat

Catapult seat

Wheel for winding in long rope with net

Chick-O-Snacks container

Rope
attached
to net

Net

Chick-O-Snack

Trying it out ... NOW! ☺

Ah.

Um.

Right.

Need to adjust the catapult seat angle. And use longer rope on the quick-release net. And get the rowing boat to collect my chicken from the ocean ...

Again.

Whoops!

Homing Chicken Training: Take Two.

She did it! She did it!!

I launched her into the sky, then cast out the fishing line with the cupcake attached. She did a neat spin in the air to try to catch the cupcake in her beak, then chased it back to the ship as I reeled in the line!

Success!! I have a genius for a chicken!!

Well ... I have a chicken.

Boris is refusing to move. Apparently she's tired out after all her hard work training!

Humph! And I don't have any more bottles to send a message to Mom.

Only option left: being "cursed and really doomed".

9a.m.

Grandpa dancing the hornpipe and finishing with a double backflip. He's clutching a *Pirating Today* newspaper.

It says:

DREAD PIRATE MADLOCKS STRIKES AGAIN

The most amazing, fearsome pirate, Dread Pirate Madlocks, has recently taken eight ships in the Port Savage area of Doom Island. Unfortunately, these include the office ship of *Pirating Today* (we're so proud—Madlocks is our hero), so there will be no more newspapers until next month.

9:30a.m.

Heading to Doom Island (that sounds
promising).

Grandpa has put me in charge of
navigation.

I'm really pleased. This is my chance to
show him what a truly excellent, fabulous
pirate I really am!

10:10a.m.

WHIRLPOOL!
WE ARE
DOOMED!!!!!!
ABANDON
SHIP!

11:30a.m.

Grandpa has put Redruth in charge of navigation.

I am now peeling potatoes for lunch. ☹

Not really my fault that the whirlpool appeared out of nowhere. Well, sort of nowhere. I suppose it did say "whirlpools be here" on my map. I just didn't realize we were on *that* bit of the map. Ahem.

3p.m.

OK, we are NOW heading toward Doom Island. Grandpa still working on a plan. Can hear him muttering the words "hopeless" and "certain death" and "Blunderbeard." Not entirely sure this is a good sign. ☹

11:30a.m.

Anchored a couple of miles away from Doom Island.

Grandpa has summoned Redruth and me to his cabin.

Hope his plan involves me staying on

board, inventing contraptions, and baking
cupcakes.

1p.m.
Nope. ☹

2p.m.
Grandpa looked through his telescope and
saw Madlocks's boat anchored
in Port Savage. He said he wished he
could get a closer look. He reckons

Madlocks is such a fearsome pirate (even by Grandpa's standards) that we need to have the element of surprise. The only way we'll stand a chance is if he doesn't know we're here.

Back in cabin. Wish I could remember where I've heard Madlocks's name before. I'm sure it's important somehow....

JULY 18ᵀᴴ

That's it!! That's IT! Even Redruth will have to admit I am a <u>complete and utter genius</u>! I have a great idea!

The SpyChick™!!!

Now Boris has got the hang of the homing instinct, she can go and spy on the ship using a special camera and report back to me. I *knew* her training would come in handy.

Everyone's a winner: Boris gets to practice her homing, Grandpa gets useful information, I get to hide under my bed.

More later. Busy being a complete and utter genius. ☺

JULY 20TH

10a.m.

Blunderbeard's WonderWeird Contraptions are

proud to present:

The SpyChick™!

Transmitter to send images back to base

Launch pad

Chicken

Video camera

Secret
microphone

Chick-O-Snacks
cupcake supply

Grandpa wasn't convinced by my plan. He grumbled on about "modern technology rubbish" and how, when he was a lad, they'd just storm a ship, take it over, and be back in time for jello and ice cream.

Redruth wasn't convinced either. She just wanted to sneak up, board the ship and blast all their hats off with her PortaCannon™.

But I've persuaded them to let me try the SpyChick™. It's a great idea. How can it possibly fail?

I'm making Redruth watch the screen with me so she can see my complete and utter genius-ness unfold before her very eyes. HA! That'll teach her.

11 a.m.

I've given "Boris the Bold" a quick ruffle of the feathers and am about to launch her.

3 … 2 … 1 … Chicks away!!

Wow. Look at her go. I'm so proud. So, SO proud.

We're watching on the screen. The plan is that she circles the boat a few times so we can look for any weaknesses that will help us capture it. Then she'll simply fly back to us undetected.

There we go. … I can see Madlocks's ship on our screen. Wow. Lots of cannons. Swords. Gunpowder. Pirates. There's the vicious dog, Whoopsie, (oh— he's a poodle) and—

Oh no. She hasn't. ... Tell me she hasn't. ...

She's landed on the ship!!

Oh. That. Chicken!! She's just wandering around all over the place. Not even in a straight line!!

Oh no. Oh, Boris, no. PLEASE, NO.

She's gone to the ship's toilet!

But those boots ... they belong to *DREAD PIRATE MADLOCKS!*

She's gone into the toilet!! And—OOOOOH! Oh dear! I won't write down the words the microphone just picked up. To be fair, it must have come as a bit of a shock to Madlocks, a chicken wandering in when you're in the middle of having a—Wait! What has she just grabbed in her beak?

Oh no. Oh, Boris, no. NOT THE

TOILET PAPER!

So *Pirate Monthly* gave Madlocks a 10/10 Awesomely Dangerous Pirate Rating. And my chicken has just run off with his toilet paper in her beak. LEAVING HIM STUCK ON THE TOILET!!!

I'm dead.

Microphone picking up Madlocks. He's bellowing for someone to get him some toilet paper RIGHT AWAY. Pirates everywhere, running around! And where's Boris going now??! She's flying up to the crow's nest! She's—

Oh no. Oh, Boris, no ... That's why she needed the toilet roll!

Right. No more ChickaPoo for Boris EVER AGAIN! ARGHH! Madlocks is furious! He's marching toward the crow's nest! With his trousers around his ankles! Oh no! Boris's poop—it's dripping on Madlocks's head!!

Argh!! The video camera battery has run out! Can hear Madlocks over the microphone. He says he's had enough. Six gold doubloons for the pirate who catches that "wretched bird" (yeek!) when they get back, but they've got to head off to the *Skull and Crossbones* at Port Savage now— they've booked a table for lunch at twelve o'clock to celebrate Madlocks winning Barber Rossa's Craziest Hair of the Year Award again. Can hear boots and doggy paws leaving the ship.

Silence. Apart from Boris … finishing off her "business." Hmm, wish the microphone had run out of battery now too.

Oh, for the love of cupcakes!!!!

Redruth laughed so much and said she was going to write to Mom and tell her all about it. In detail.

What do I do now??!! I can't leave Boris stuck on that ship, to be made into pot pie. ☹ And if Grandpa finds out what a disaster this is, he will go crazier than Blackbeard did that time I put a crab in his pants.

I've got to rescue Boris, and I've got to do it now.

Well … I guess all the pirates are off the ship.…

I could just *borrow* Grandpa's rowing boat again.…

And hope I survive.

OH. THAT. CHICKEN!!!!

12p.m.
I want a parrot instead!!!!!!

Left a note for Grandpa and Redruth explaining I've gone to rescue a rogue homing chicken and I might be late for supper (and don't let Redruth eat my dessert).

1p.m.
Pulled up the rowing boat beside Madlocks's ship. Can see Boris up in the crow's nest. No sign of pirates anywhere.

If I don't make it back, and this is my last entry, let it be known that brave young Blunderbeard perished on his quest to save his fearless, formerly constipated chicken, Boris the Bold, from being made into pot pie by the very fearsome Dread Pirate Madlocks.

(Let it also be known that it was
Redruth who stole all the chocolate
cookies. Sorry, Grandpa, she swore me to
secrecy.)

1:15p.m.
Am on board.

Has just occurred to me: <u>I have done it</u>!
I, Blunderbeard, am on board Madlocks's
ship! ME!!

Ha! I name myself CAPTAIN
BARNACLES BLUNDERBEARD,
Captain of the *Laughing Skull* (at least
for a few minutes), with a *Pirate Monthly*
Awesomely Dangerous Pirate Rating of

10/10! Brave explorer, expert sailor, rescuer of chickens in distress!

Hey, I've got a few minutes. Feel I should rescue Boris in style and try out some of my pirate training moves. Grandpa would be proud. And at least all those awful lessons won't have been for nothing.

I'll climb up some rigging, swing across to the main mast on that loose rope, then drop neatly into the crow's nest to grab Boris.

Here I go!!

OUCH.

That would be the main mast.

Climbing up into crow's nest ...
ARGH!

Stepped right into a huge pile of chicken poop! Can't believe I forgot about that. ☹ Will take me ages to clean these boots. Oh well. Lucky there's some toilet paper left on the roll ...

Going to grab Boris and swing back on the rope.

OUCH.

The other mast. OK, so ropes aren't my thing.
Moving on ...

1:19p.m.

Ooh, there's the captain's cabin. Dashing
inside.

Any clues? Any weaknesses? Even a
10/10 pirate must have a weakness! If I can
find it, Grandpa will be so proud of me.

Wait a minute! Look! *Captain Cook's
Recipe Book: Volume 2: More Cakes*! I've got
Volume One on Grandpa's ship. Not seen
a Volume Two before. Madlocks must like
his cakes, just like me. Ooh, this looks really

good. Crunchy crab and raisin scones on page twenty-eight. Argh. Boris pulling at my sleeve with her beak. Get off! Daft chicken. Ooh: page thirty-three, seaweed sponge cake. Boris, stop it! She probably needs the toilet again, unless—

Uh-oh.

The sound of boots.

And tough, piratey voices.

HELP! We're going to be caught unless I think of a plan!!

1:21p.m.

Thought of a plan.

Boris and I are hiding in a large lidded basket in a corner of the cabin.

It was a clever plan. Until I realized this is Dread Pirate Madlocks's dirty laundry bin! The smell is AWFUL! And Boris keeps fidgeting next to me. Don't know *what* she's doing!! Ooh, look—Madlocks sews little nametags into his underpants.

Removing the SpyChick™ equipment from Boris, just in case we get caught.

SSSSHHHH! Madlocks is coming in, with another pirate! Stuffed Boris's beak in a dirty sock to keep her quiet.

This is what they're saying:

"And you STILL haven't ordered some more special glue for my ... well ... for the *you-know-what*."

"Sorry, Captain, Your Dreadfulness, sir. I'll do it today. Your secret's safe with me."

"Better had be, Bones. Or you're walkin' the plank. And you don't want to be doin' that."

"Nay, Captain, Your Dreadfulness, sir."

Gulp.

Guess we'll be waiting in here until he's gone, then. Surely he won't be long.

3:20p.m.
Still waiting.

So nervous am biting my nails again.

<u>Really</u> need to pee. ☹

And this laundry bin smells worse than Grandpa's aftershave.

4:20p.m.
Worried the sound of chewing fingernails is too noisy. Putting Madlocks's stinky socks on my hands to stop me biting nails.

GOOD GRIEF! Boris is actually wearing a pair of Madlocks's underwear!

How on the Seven Seas did she—? Never mind. At least Madlocks doesn't know about it. Don't think pirates like chickens wearing their underpants. But we're safe. He has NO idea we're here—

Oh no. Oh very VERY no. Boris's beak is twitching. Her nostrils are smoking. We are DOOMED!! It's really not good when a chicken who is part-dragon lets out an enormous—

JULY 21ST

Oh. That. CHICKEN!!

Great. JUST GREAT.

Boris *bloomin'* Flamebeak SNEEZED.

The laundry bin whooshed up in the air
and burst into flames.

The sock on her beak caught fire and
went flying across the room.

The bin landed in a pile of ash.

We crashed in a heap at Madlocks's feet.

The fiery sock landed on a piece of

paper Madlocks was holding.

It burned to a crisp.

As I looked up at him, trying to give him my best smile, I remembered that Boris was wearing his underpants. And I was wearing his socks on my hands. Things were not going to go well.

His eyes went wide and he tugged his curls in rage and yelled "Toilet roll!"

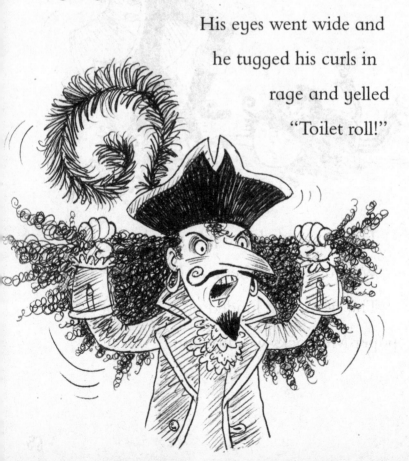

several times and jumped up and down.
Madlocks sent Boris to the kitchen. He's
saving her to be made into chicken pot pie
for his birthday meal. ☹

Madlocks asked me what a boy and a
chicken were doing near his ship. I wouldn't
tell him, but then he threatened to make
me dance the hornpipe until dawn. So
I just said I'd come from Grandpa's ship
which was anchored nearby, and my
chicken had flown off and got lost, and
I was trying to get her back (technically,
all true). Then Madlocks held a "Sink
Blunderbeard's Rowing Boat" competition
with this crew. Then he sent his parrot with
a note to Grandpa's ship saying that he

knew Grandpa was there and that rather than making me walk the plank, he'd decided to keep me on board because he had a use for me.

What use?

Well, I'm in the laundry room. Turns out the other pirates hate doing Madlocks's washing as it smells AWFUL. So he's making ME do it as a punishment. My hands will stink forever. ☹

Grandpa's Proper Pirate Training never said anything about whiffy underpants.

I demand a refund.

Pirates **A**gainst **R**ubbish **P**iracy **S**ociety

The Best Pirate Ship in the World

Dead Man's Cove

The Ocean

July 22ND

Dear Tiresome, Stupid, Complete Little Idiot of a Brother,

PARPS has recently received a letter from Pirate Madlocks informing us that your pirate pet, Boris Flamebeak the ridiculous chicken, has been responsible for stealing a captain's toilet paper and insulting him.

WHAT IS THE MATTER WITH YOU??????!!!!!!!

Perhaps you are unaware that Dread Pirate Madlocks is top of our list to be the new patron of PARPS? Although I told you TWENTY TIMES last year.

Perhaps you are also unaware that, even among pirates, it is not considered "acceptable" for your pet to steal someone's toilet paper when they're using the toilet! ESPECIALLY when it's DREAD PIRATE MADLOCKS! Who your big brother is trying DESPERATELY to recruit to be the new patron of PARPS! IN CASE YOU

MISSED IT THE FIRST TWENTY-ONE
TIMES!

This is your last warning, Blunderbeard, or
else I WILL come and get you ... to personally
throw you overboard to Davy Jones's Locker!

Yours sincerely, in a really bad mood with
you,

Blasterous Blackbeard

(Director of PARPS)

Ah. That'll be why the name was familiar,
then. Whoops. ☹

Argh! Something whizzing toward the laundry-room window!

Landed in the washing barrel and splashed dirty washing water all over my face.

Fished it out.

Cannonball wrapped in hot-pink paper.

Only one person communicates like this: Redruth. The PortaCannon™ I made for her is really accurate over long distances.

Maybe she and Grandpa have a rescue

plan! Maybe they're coming to get me—
I'm saved! ☺

    Oh.

    Not exactly. ☹

The Breath O'Death

The Ocean

Hey, Blunders,

Yoooooooooooooooooou idiot. Boy,
are you in trouble. Again. Grandpa is
soooooo not happy with you. You've
gone and ruined our surprise attack! Now
they know we're here, they'll be keep-
ing an eye on Grandpa's ship! He says
you'd better find another way that

we can catch them off guard. If you don't, he's going to send you back to the Island of No Return and feed you to his pet shark, Colin. That's if Madlocks doesn't get you first. Or Blackbeard. Actually, Blunders, there's quite a list. Oh, and Grandpa says don't bother trying to escape the *Laughing Skull* and swim back. He says he's not letting you on board again until we've got Madlocks's ship.

Soooooo totally glad I'm not you. Have fun!

Laters,
R xxx

OK, OK, keep calm.

All I have to do is to figure out how to save my chicken from being made into a birthday pot pie, come up with a plan to take over this ship which is packed with horrible pirates, and hand it over to Grandpa before my hands stink for eternity. Easy. ☹

PANIC!!!!!!!!!!!!!!!!

OK, deep breaths ... There must be a way out of this.

I'm sure I'll think of something. For now I'll just keep my head down ... stay out of trouble ... finish off this load of washing and—

Hang on.

Oh dear. Oh very VERY dear.

Is that a red sock in with Madlocks's
white shirts?

Mail. ☹

Pirates **A**gainst **R**ubbish **P**iracy **S**ociety

The Best Pirate Ship in the World

Dead Man's Cove

The Ocean

July 26th

PINK, BLUNDERBEARD?! YOU DYED ALL

HIS WHITE SHIRTS PINK???!!

SORT. IT. OUT!

Yours in deepest despair

at your unbelievable

stupidity,

Blasterous Blackbeard

(Director of PARPS)

JULY 30TH

10a.m.

Am now banned from doing the laundry, and have been put on dusting duty. Madlocks has a LOT of trophies.

No problem.

10:12a.m.

Ohhhhhh dear.

I just wanted to make sure everything was really clean so I wouldn't get in trouble. Especially Madlocks's CRAZIEST HAIR OF THE YEAR AWARD. He loves that trophy.

Dusted it a bit. Knocked it off the shelf a bit. It smashed … a bit.

Now it's missing

a head.

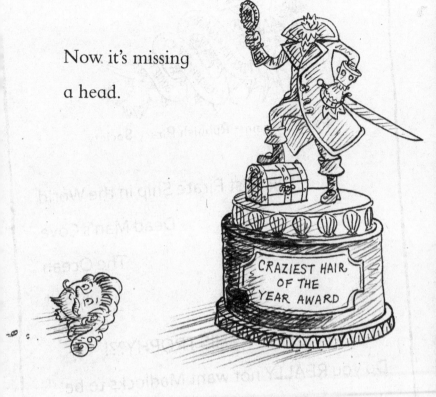

CRAZIEST HAIR
OF THE
YEAR AWARD

Think I might soon be missing mine as

well. ☹

JULY 31ST

I hate mail.

Pirates **A**gainst **R**ubbish **P**iracy **S**ociety

The Best Pirate Ship in the World

Dead Man's Cove

The Ocean

July 30th

YOU DID <u>WHAT</u> TO HIS TROPHY??!
Do you REALLY not want Madlocks to be
the patron of PARPS??!! He is FURIOUS
with you. SO Am I.

Yours so very EXTREMELY
crossly there aren't words
I am allowed to use,

Blasterous Blackbeard
(Director of PARPS)

Yes. Well. Moving on. Am now on kitchen duty.

I need to:

1. Think of a plan to take over this ship.
2. Rescue doomed chicken.
3. ~~Get on with the laundry.~~
4. ~~Do the dusting.~~
5. Stay out of trouble.
6. Make dessert.

Actually, to save time, I'll be realistic:

1. Think of a plan to take over this ship.
2. Rescue doomed chicken.
3. ~~Get on with the laundry.~~
4. ~~Do the dusting.~~
5. ~~Stay out of trouble.~~ (forget it)
6. Make dessert.

At least I'm in the kitchen now and can keep an eye on Boris. They've chained her up but are feeding her Chick-O-Snacks so that she's nice and fat for the birthday feast. She's really happy about it. She doesn't know about the pot pie. ☹

AUGUST 9TH

PLAN TO CONQUER THE LAUGHING SKULL:
OPERATION SHIP SNATCH

OPERATION SHIP SNATCH: PLAN A:
Arrange a swimming race so that all the pirates are in the water, then signal to Grandpa and Redruth to get on board and sail off with ship before they come back.

Asked Madlocks if I could send a note to Grandpa reminding him to water my cactus (sssh, pretend!).

Madlocks said no.

I said I'd bake him some lemon cupcakes.

Madlocks said yes.

He told me to give the note to one of his crew members to deliver so I chose Lazy Jim. I know Lazy Jim can't read because I saw him holding a copy of *Pirate Monthly* upside down.

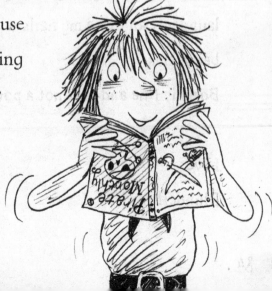

This is what my note really said:

TOP SECRET

Dear Grandpa and Redruth,

I have a great plan. Tomorrow I'm organizing
a swimming race for the crew. When you hear
me blow the whistle, bring your rowing boat
and we'll take over the ship.

I am fine, although my fingers still stink from
laundry. Can't bite my nails without nearly
being sick.

Boris is fine and still not a pot pie.

Love,
Blunderbeard

10a.m.

Well, here we go!

Turned up on deck, wearing only my swimming trunks and a pink-swan rubber ring around my waist (it was the only one I could find).

When all the pirates stopped laughing at me (humph), they asked why I was dressed like that.

I explained that today is National Pirate Swimming Race Day— didn't they know about it? It's the latest thing.

Madlocks said of course he already knew about the race because he was the coolest pirate around—*Pirate Monthly* and *PUS* had told him so. He pretended he was waiting for the rest of the crew, and now he's gone off to get changed. All the other pirates have copied him.

I'm going to stay on deck and blow the whistle to start the race.

10:15a.m.

They're all ready. Madlocks is wearing a swimming cap—he says his hair is too fabulous and important to get wet.

Blew the whistle.

Peered through my telescope.

Can just see Grandpa and Redruth getting into the rowing boat and heading this way.

Success will be mine.

AUGUST 19TH

Ohhhhhhhhhhh dear.

Failure is mine.

Turns out a swimming race and angry, ferocious, giant man-eating eels don't go well together.

I'm banned from organizing any sport activities ever again. On the plus side, I've

NEVER seen pirates swim that fast. Very
impressive.

Peered through the telescope. Saw
Grandpa and Redruth quickly rowing

back to their ship. Grandpa was waving his

fist in my direction and didn't look happy.

Madlocks also ordered me to bake

cupcakes for everyone to say sorry.

He's very, very angry. ☹

HOW ON THE SEVEN SEAS ARE
WE GOING TO GET THIS SHIP??!!

My birthday. At least I baked a cupcake to
cheer myself up.

Did I get a birthday card from my dear
brother? Nope. But I did get this. ☹

Pirates **A**gainst **R**ubbish **P**iracy **S**ociety

The Best Pirate Ship in the World

Dead Man's Cove

The Ocean

August 19th

Blunderbeard,

SWIMMING RACE??!! EEL-INFESTED
WATERS??!! PINK SWAN RUBBER
RING ??!! ARE YOU OUT OF YOUR TINY,
TINY BRAIN?

Not only has Madlocks complained to

me AGAIN, but Captain Harry Chomp of S.M.E.L.L.S. (Society for Monsters Existing in Large Lakes and Seas) has written to me and I quote:

"Those giant man-eating eels were only released into the wild last week. The poor things are shy enough as it is without YOUR LITTLE BROTHER setting up a ridiculous swimming race to scare them to bits! Do you know how hard it is to calm down a stressed-out giant man-eating eel? Do you? I have been bitten eighty-three times and slapped around the face twice. I've had to around them all up, keep them in a huge, dark tank, and feed them chamomile tea. Do you know how hard it

is to persuade a giant man-eating eel
that it wants to drink chamomile tea?!
DO YOU?!"

If you don't find a way to make it up to Madlocks, I WILL NOT invite you to my birthday party (though you still have to make me that really huge, rum-flavored birthday cupcake, because you promised).

Yours, about to explode,

Blasterous Blackbeard
(Director of PARPS)
P.S. "Happy" birthday.

Oh dear.

Maybe Blackbeard should try drinking chamomile tea in a dark tank.

2p.m.

Just when I thought the day couldn't get any worse:

Madlocks said he and the other pirates had had a meeting. They're fed up with me causing trouble and are making me walk the plank. I'll have to leave Boris behind and swim back to Grandpa and explain I'm a complete and utter failure. Again.

3p.m.

On the plank.

I'm doomed. ☹

Farewell, cruel ship. Farewell, cruel pirates. Farewell, cruel world.

4p.m.

Not doomed.

As I walked the plank, I told the pirates they were being especially mean as it was my birthday. No one should have to walk the plank on their birthday.

Then Madlocks said, "Shiver me timbers, boy!! I knows what ye mean! 'Tis me birthday soon and none of this rotten crew's done anything about it!"

Aha, thinks I. Maybe I won't have to walk the plank.

"You poor pirate," I said. "Instead of kicking me off your ship, why don't you let me plan your party?"

Madlocks clapped his hands together and gave a little bounce. "Deal!" he roared.

REEEEEEEESULT.

AUGUST 21ST

OPERATION SHIP SNATCH: PLAN B
And we're back on track!

Tomorrow I'm arranging for them to practice "Sleeping Sharks" for one of Madlocks's party games. So they will all lie down as quietly as they can, WITHOUT MOVING (that part's quite important) and I'll be the one to call "Out!" if I see anyone move. The last one "in" is the winner. Except I'll trick them! I won't call anyone "out" for ages—well, not until I've lowered the flag on the ship and Grandpa and Redruth are on board and tying up the other pirates with rope.

It's a perfect plan!

10a.m.
Sent Lazy Jim with a note to Grandpa and Redruth. Pretended it was a note asking them to renew my library book.

But really it said:

TOP SECRET

Dear Grandpa and Redruth,

Whoops.

Giant man-eating eels... angry pirates...

chamomile tea... plank-walking...

Aaaaaaaaaanyway...

Change of plan.

When you see me lower the *Laughing Skull*

flag, come across as quickly as you can.

I am well and Boris is fat.

Love,

Blunderbeard

AUGUST 22ND

11a.m.

The whole crew of the *Laughing Skull* are lying face down on the deck. Being silent, still, and very, very un-piratey. They are all determined to win because no pirate wants to be a loser. And because I've offered a dozen lime-and-coconut cupcakes for the winner.

11:03a.m.

This is awesome. The ship will be ours!

Am lowering the flag. Grandpa and Redruth will be on their way any moment.

Doing a quick (and quiet) victory dance.

Go, Blunders! Go, Blunders! Go—

11:15a.m.

Oh no. Oh VERY no. ☹

Turns out it's rather difficult to do a quick, quiet victory dance with pirates lying all over the deck. Trod on Lazy Jim (he's very good at "Sleeping Sharks").

Wobbled.

Which made me trip over Bones.

Which made me fall backwards over Peggy Pegleg.

Which made me land SPLAT on Dread Pirate Madlocks, nearly knocking off his hat.

He was ... er ... shall we say, *a little bit put out*. Apparently, no one in the history of pirates has EVER DARED to touch his hat before. I can see why. He went as red as a boiled lobster from yelling so much. Wonder why he's so angry about his hat coming off? Come to think of it, I've never seen him without some sort of hat before.

Anyway, then all the pirates started arguing about who won and was going to get the cupcakes.

I quietly hoisted the flag again. Saw Grandpa and Redruth rowing back. Grandpa was jumping up and down in the boat. Glad I can't lip-read very well. ☹

Going back to the kitchen to make a dozen lime-and-coconut cupcakes for EVERYONE. ☹

New Rule: stop opening envelopes.

Pirates **A**gainst **R**ubbish **P**iracy **S**ociety

The Best Pirate Ship in the World

Dead Man's Cove

The Ocean

August 23RD

BLUNDERBEARD!

HIS HAT?! YOU TOUCHED HIS HAT?!

DO YOU NOT WANT TO LIVE ANY MORE?!

I've asked him to give you one more chance before he makes you walk the plank. ONE CHANCE, Blunderbeard, and that's it. And if he DOES make you walk the plank, I'm coming to watch.

Yours, jumping up and down on my pirate hat really crossly <u>BECAUSE OF YOU</u>,

Blasterous Blackbeard

(Director of PARPS)

AUGUST 26TH

OPERATION SHIP SNATCH: PLAN C

Get the pirates to make some birthday
bunting from an old sail. When we're holding
it ready to tie into place, I'll quickly spring
into action and tie them all up instead! Then
Grandpa and Redruth can come and storm
the ship. Easy as (not chicken) pie.

Sent Lazy Jim with a note to Grandpa.
Pretended I was checking if my
GunkMelter™ toenail-cleaner machine
is unplugged. (Haven't really invented
the GunkMelter™—well, not yet—after
sharing Blackbeard's cabin a few years ago,
it's DEFINITELY in the cards.)

The note really said:

TOP SECRET

Dear Grandpa and Annoying Cousin,

I've got another great plan.

Bunting is my secret weapon. Who needs swords and cannons??

When you see the *Laughing Skull*'s flag lowered, please come and take over the ship.

I am well and Boris is even fatter.

Love,

Blunderbeard

AUGUST 27TH

Ohhhhhhhh dear.

It all started so well. They made the bunting and decorated it nicely. I lowered the flag to give Grandpa and Redruth time to get here.

I held the bunting up for everyone to see, about to spring into action with my cunning plan …

And then everything went wrong!

First, the pirates all squabbled about whose piece of bunting was prettiest.

Then they all squabbled about whose piece of bunting was biggest.

Then they all squabbled about whose piece of bunting was strongest.

I tried to stop them but was pushed out of the way, with my back against the mast. The pirates all rushed around crossly, arguing and tugging the bunting in every direction … Left, right … round and round …

Grandpa and Redruth arrived just in time to see me tied to the mast with a piece of bunting dangling over my face.

I blew it out of the way and saw Grandpa glaring at me and Redruth taking a photo as they rowed back to their ship again. She'll probably send that photo to Blackbeard. Dratted girl! May all her freckles turn into pimples!!

OPERATION SHIP SNATCH: PLAN D

Er …

Um …

Hmm ...

~~OPERATION SHIP SNATCH~~

OPERATION TOTAL DISASTER: PLAN D

Go back to Grandpa's ship, minus a fat chicken, and get forced to walk the plank.

Done. ☹

10a.m.

Incoming pink cannonball!

Demolished trifle.

Splattered ship.

No dessert for hungry pirates.

And it knocked my diary into the
dishwater.

Sigh.

Now what does she want?

Hey, Blunders.

Just so you know, Grandpa is getting really impatient. He says if you don't make the arrangements for us getting this ship really soon, he's sooooo going to throw all your *Blunderbeard WonderWeird Contraptions* and your cake recipe books into the sea.
Suits me. I can use them for target practice.
Take your time.

Laters,
R xxx

No! Not my HenHomer™!
And my PatchPolisher™! And my
BeardWringer™—I'd nearly got that to
work without ripping off your beard!

And my recipe books! I had a special
recipe I wanted to use for Blackbeard's
stupid birthday cake and—

WAIT!

TA-DAAAHHH! Complete and utter
genius-ness strikes again!

I've figured out Madlocks's weak spot—
and I've had an excellent idea! Grandpa is
going to be so impressed. What we need to
do is distract Madlocks and his scary crew
with something amazing so Grandpa and
Redruth can sneak aboard, yes?

And I know just how to distract them.

11a.m.

Have offered to make Madlocks's birthday cake the biggest and best one he has <u>ever</u> had. He agreed. I said I needed my *Extra Extra Strong Baking Powder for Cakes* from Grandpa's ship.

Sent Lazy Jim with this note. It said:

TOP SECRET

Dear Grandpa and Redruth,

Plan D! I have it!

Please send over my *Extra Extra Strong Baking Powder for Cakes* with Lazy Jim.

I'm going to bake a huge, amazing cake for Madlocks. While the pirates are amazed and astounded and digging in, we'll catch them unawares and take over the ship! Listen for me ringing the ship's bell.

I am fine and Boris is ginormous.

Love,

Blunderbeard

2p.m.

My diary is still soggy from the dishwater.
There are bubbles on March 10th!

Have a plan: the DiaryDryer™! This
will also come in handy for whenever I
accidentally drop my diary in the sea/
bath/toilet.

Large handle
for me to turn
(when Boris
isn't around)

Large wheel for Boris to run in
(when Boris is about)

Chick-O-Snack dispenser

Huge
Bellows

Stand for
diary/hat/pants
whatever needs
drying

I've now got my baking powder and other supplies. This plan had better work.

If it doesn't, there's no time now to come up with another one. ☹

Ingredients:

1 barrel of flour

1 barrel of sugar

1 barrel of margarine

However many eggs I can get from Boris in the next few days

10 bars of chocolate

4 bottles of peppermint oil

1 WHOLE JAR of *Extra Extra Strong Baking Powder for Really Big Cakes*

(Need to be careful with that. The baking powder really, REALLY doesn't mix well with fire and was the reason my ship sank last year, through no fault of my own. Anyway ... more later. I need to make a birthday cake!)

SEPTEMBER 3RD

10a.m.
Baking.

2p.m.
Still baking.

4p.m.

Fed up with baking. Pleeeeeeeeeeeeeeeeease
let my plan work.

7p.m.

Decorating the biggest, most amazing,
mint chocolate birthday cake the world
has ever seen. This, ladies and gentlemen, is
our secret weapon. Barnacles Blunderbeard
will conquer the ship of the Dread Pirate
Madlocks ... with a cake!

9a.m.

Madlocks's birthday!

Time to put my magnificent plan into action.

This will be great. They're going to be so amazed by the cake, and all stuffing their faces so they won't even notice Grandpa and Redruth boarding the ship.

What could possibly go wrong?

Actually ... let's not go there.

Still something's nagging at the back of my mind like a great, big ... nagging thing.

What have I forgotten?

10a.m.

PARTY TIME!!

Madlocks said he's spent three hours
getting his hair to look just perfect for the
party! (And I thought Redruth was bad.)

The pirates wanted to play "Musical
Thumps." So when the accordion stops …
you thump the nearest pirate before they
thump you. I'm making them stop because
Bones has been bopped on the nose and
started to cry.

Perhaps a nice,
quiet game of
"Pin the Hook
on the Pirate."

10:15a.m.

Nope! Bad idea.

Just unpinning Lazy Jim from the mast …

11a.m.

Time to do the treasure hunt. I've hidden some little chocolate gold coins all over the ship. Surely that should keep them out of trouble for five minutes.

11:15a.m.

For the love of cupcakes! Whenever anyone found any "treasure," all the pirates fought to claim it for themselves!!

Had to get very firm with the crew. Have now made everyone sit down in a circle with their arms folded, their legs crossed, and their fingers on their lips.

I've said they have to be quiet and behave themselves for ONE MINUTE (one minute—that's all I ask!) and *then* they can play pass the parcel.

11:16a.m.
Making them stay quiet for another minute because they all giggled when Peggy Pegleg belched.

11:17a.m.
Right. NOW we can play pass the parcel.

I'm playing the accordion and they can

open a layer of the parcel when I stop.

Simple, right?

11:23a.m.

… Unless the parcel stops RIGHT between two pirates, and they can't agree which one should get it.

Massive swordfight … four pirates
overboard … and somehow the parcel got
loaded into a cannon and fired out into
the middle of the sea.

Where it was gobbled up by a giant
man-eating (and parcel-eating) eel.

Guess Captain Chomp has let them
out again. Don't suppose he'll be pleased
to discover one's just eaten a musical
telescope.

12p.m.

Party food! Thank goodness! Should be
harder for them to yell and squabble with
their mouths full of food.

12:05p.m.

OK, make that "party-food fight."

Am ducking the tuna sandwiches and
prawn cocktail potato chips flying across
the table.

AAAARGH! Madlocks just threw orange punch all over Peggy Pegleg and got my diary wet too! Not happy!!!!!!

Have now taken DiaryDryer™ on deck to dry diary after I've served cake (humph). And now for the giant birthday cake!!!

Just poking the candles in. It looks delicious.

About to carry it up to the deck now. Here we go!

I can see Grandpa and Redruth! They've tucked their rowing boat next to the *Laughing Skull*. Redruth has her PortaCannon™ and Grandpa has his trusty sword.

What do I have? An oversized cake and a fat chicken chained up in a kitchen.

Grandpa and Redruth are ready to storm the ship.

My heart's thumping.

This had better work.

If only I could remember that thing I've forgotten ... .

Right, lighting the candles NOW.

Clearing my throat, ready to sing.

"Happy birthday to you ..." all the pirates have stopped throwing the crab puffs and are joining in. Excellent. I have their attention. Any moment now, Grandpa and Redruth will spring into action ...

WAIT! The thing bugging me at the back of my mind!

The *Extra Extra Strong Baking Powder ...* explosive ... blew up my ship ... keep away from fire ...

CANDLES!!!!!!!!!

OH NO—I'm going to blow up the ship!

Must knock cake overboard!

AAAAAAAAAARGH!!!!!

BOOM.

It exploded in mid-air—cake is flying everywhere!

Madlocks says he loves the fireworks!

Now all the pirates are scrambling to get the cake!

Right—this is it! Ringing the bell! Getting a few odd looks.

Now singing "Happy Birthday" as I ring the bell. They seem very pleased with that and are stuffing more cake into their mouths.

Grandpa and Redruth are aboard.

The fight for the ship is on!

12:20p.m.

Redruth's PortaCannon™ is going off somewhere—hats flying in all directions. Can hear her whooping. Sounds like she's having a great time.

Grandpa is fighting about three of Madlocks's crew—oh, and managing to eat cake and cartwheel at the same time.

I should probably help him … but, well …
fighting has never been my strong point.
And everything looks under control here …
If "control" is utter, utter chaos. Time to
find Boris.

Let "Operation Big Bird" begin!

12:25p.m.

Trying to dodge the barrels which are
crashing across the decks. Can hear
Grandpa cheering. Don't think he's had
this much fun in ages.

In the kitchen. There's Boris the Huge!

Good grief. She looks like a feathery
football with legs.

Sorry, Madlocks, chicken pot pie's off the menu!

Come on, Boris—pull at the chains!

She's just looking at me and burping. She'd rather sit here getting fed and getting fat.

PULL AT THE CHAINS, BORIS!

Oh. That. CHICKEN!

AHA! The pirates have left the Chick-O-Snacks on the table. All I need to do is leave a little trail of them. She's straining to reach them. Anything for Chick-O-Snacks! She's pulling and yanking …

She's snapped the chains!

Right, grabbed Boris—now back up to find Grandpa and Redruth.

12:28a.m.

YEEK!

All the pirates are fighting each other now! I think they've forgotten who or what they were fighting about in the first place and are just having a jolly good time.

Just heard Madlocks bellow that this is the best birthday party he's ever had and he loves the "party entertainment." TRIPLE YEEK! Redruth just blew Grandpa's hat off! No dessert for her tonight, then.

Boris? Boris, what are you doing? COME BACK!

She's running through the crowd … she's … she's seen my DiaryDryer™! She's climbing in! She must have sniffed out the Chick-O-Snacks!

She's gobbling loads of Chick-O-Snacks! She's in overdrive! Boris! Slow down!

She's blowing up a mighty breeze! Everyone's stopped to find out where the breeze is coming from. The last remaining hats are tumbling overboard, except Madlocks's. He's clinging to his like crazy.

OH NO! Here comes Madlocks, marching toward us. WE'VE HAD IT!

Hang on, I've got an idea. He really doesn't want his hat to come off, does he?

Why not? What's he hiding? Let's find out!!

QUICK! Turning dial to HURRICANE TURBO setting. Pointing it right at Madlocks!

AAARGH! Strong—wind! Madlocks—yelling.

Am—clinging— to—mast.

Madlocks's hat—blown off!—and
now—hair blown off!—was wig!—now
bald head!

Everyone gasping—Redruth giggling.

Tattoo on head—"I LOVE MOMMY".

Phew! The breeze has stopped. Boris is so stuffed, she's fallen asleep.

Everyone staring at Madlocks.

ABSOLUTE STUNNED SILENCE ON DECK. (Until Boris starts snoring.)

No more winning Barber Rossa's Craziest Hair Awards for him.

Now's my big moment. I know JUST what to do to save the day.

Ready.
Set.
GO!

5p.m.

So, what happened?

Well, it was my big moment. I remembered all of Grandpa's Proper Pirate Training and decided I'd better make an entrance. I grabbed one of the ropes and started swinging.

I was aiming to land in the crow's nest.
I missed, swung across the deck and
knocked over two pirates. Then the rope
twisted around the mast, and I swung into it
head-first with an almighty WALLOP and
fell to the ground in a heap. Ow. My. Head.

Everyone was watching me. So I got dizzily to my feet and wobbled over to Madlocks.

"Madlocks, Grandpa is writing *Proper Pirating for Beginners: Volume 3*," I said, as the ship began to spin around me.

The pirates all went "ooh" and gave Grandpa the thumbs-up. Oh. Grandpa has a fan club.

"AND," I continued, seeing double everywhere, "he will write your entry and tell EVERYONE about your tattoo and that your hair isn't real."

The pirates all went "ooh" again.

"That is, unless you give this ship back to Grandpa," I said, wondering why Madlocks had grown two heads. "You took it from him and he wants it back NOW."

Actually, Blunders, you were getting really dizzy from the bump on your head by then. That might be what you MEANT to say. Kinda came out "You. Ship. Grandpa. Two heads! Two heads! NOW." and then you passed out.

Shut up, Redruth, this is my story, OK? Get out of my diary and find me an ice pack or something helpful.

Idiot.

OK, so if anyone asks how I got the big bump on my head, I'll mention fighting Madlocks, and maybe just skip the details. The point is—we GOT THE SHIP! Madlocks blamed Bones for not ordering the special wig glue in time and said Bones had to get him a really good birthday present to make up for it. Like a new ship.

We left them all on Doom Island. Madlocks was really angry but I still think he had a birthday to remember. And we let them take the rest of the birthday cake. We are now sailing the *Breath O'Death* <u>and</u> the *Laughing Skull* back to Dead Man's Cove as I write. Grandpa was really

proud and said I'd finally learned a thing
or two about pirating.

Sort of...

DECEMBER 1ST

Grandpa is taking us back to Dead Man's
Cove in time for a family Christmas, but
he won't stay. He says he needs some time
to write *Proper Pirating for Beginners: Volume
3* now.

And recover from having us on board for
a year.

He'll keep in touch though, and pop in
from time to time. It'll be odd going back
to Dead Man's Cove, but I'm sure another

adventure will turn up.

DECEMBER 31ST

Back in Dead Man's Cove.

Christmas was

"interesting,"

especially when

Boris decided to

be the fairy on

top of the

tree.

Mom gave me a new hat and Blackbeard gave me a new bottle of ChickaPoo. Grumph.

And Redruth stuck this note in my diary:

Hey Blunders!

Thought you'd like to hear the good news. As Dad's busy looking after the treasure on the Island of No Return, your mom said I can stay with you. Bet you're sooooo happy.
This is gonna be fun!!

Laters,
R xxx

Well, THAT will be something to look forward to.

Time to think about my New Year's resolutions. This year, for the first time EVER, I don't have to think about stopping biting my nails. (Yuck. I'm never doing that again!!)

So here are my resolutions:

1. Prove to my big brother Blackbeard once and for all that I am NOT a waste of space.

2. Teach Boris a special new skill.

3. Do something awesome and make it into *Pirate Monthly*—well, why not?

4. Find a way to get rid of Redruth.

Wish me luck! ☺

THE END

Don't miss Pirate Blunderbeard and Boris's
first adventure....

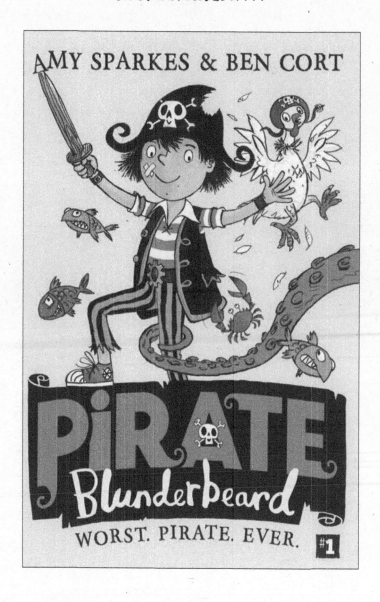

Dare you join Pirate Blunderbeard and Boris
on the Island of No Return?

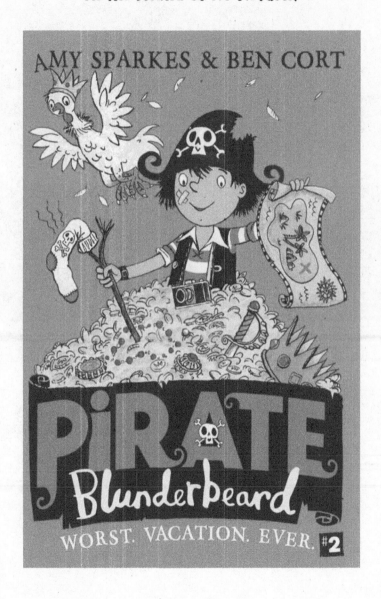